THE THREE LITTLE PIGS

Copyright © 1994, 1995 Shogo Hirata. Originally published by Joie, Inc.
Copyright © 1994, 1995 Modern Publishing, a division of Unisystems, Inc.
™ Fun-To-Read Fairy Tales is a trademark owned by Modern Publishing, a division of Unisystems, Inc.
All Rights Reserved.
® Honey Bear Books is a trademark owned by Honey Bear Productions, Inc., and is registered in the U.S. Patent
and Trademark Office. No part of this book may be reproduced or copied in any format without written
permission from the publisher. All Rights Reserved. Printed in the U.S.A.

Modern Publishing
A Division of Unisystems, Inc./New York, New York 10022

Once upon a time there were three little pigs named Elmer, Hubert and Pete, who lived with their mother in the country.

One day, Mother Pig said to her sons, "You are old enough now to have your own homes, so you must build them.

"Your father built this house out of plaster, wood and stone, and it is a good house, strong against the weather and sturdy, so that no wolf will ever break into it. Build your houses as your father did his, good and strong and sturdy, and you will always be safe and well. Remember, hard work pays off!"

The eldest pig, Elmer, was lazy. He did not want to lift heavy things to build his home. So he decided to build his house out of hay.

"Surely hay is plenty good enough to protect me from rain and from little old wolves," he said. His brother was not so sure.

"It doesn't look strong enough to me," said Pete.

"I will build my house out of sticks. Sticks don't weigh that much," said Hubert, who was also lazy, "but they are stronger than hay."

Hubert was just finishing his house of sticks when Pete, the youngest brother, happened by with a load of bricks.

"What are those for?" asked Hubert.

"For my house," answered Pete.

"You don't need to work with heavy bricks to build a house. Why, a stick house is plenty strong enough against the weather and any old wolf who might come by," said Hubert.

"Maybe so," said Pete. "But I want to build the best, strongest, sturdiest house I can, and I think it should be made out of bricks. Hard work pays off!"

"Crazy pig," muttered Elmer and Hubert as they watched Pete work long into the night to finish his house. "So much work for no good reason!"

Pete didn't listen. He kept on working, and
soon his brick house was finished.

The next day, the three little pigs moved into their new homes.

That night, Hubert and Pete walked Elmer home. They didn't know that a wolf was lurking nearby. Elmer bragged about his new house and how much easier his was to build than his brothers'.

"It's as strong as steel!" he bragged.

"I think my stick house is even stronger!" claimed Hubert. "I dare any wolf to try and break into my house!"

"Me, too!" cried Elmer.

"We'll see about that!" the wolf giggled to himself.

That night, the wolf went to Elmer's house.

"Little pig, little pig, let me in."

"Not by the hairs of my chinny-chin-chin," wailed Elmer. But the wolf huffed and puffed and blew the house down!

Elmer ran as fast as he could to Hubert's house.

No sooner had Elmer warned
Hubert that the wolf was near,
than a tremendous banging shook
the door of Hubert's stick house.

"Let me in, little pigs, let me
in," the wolf sang. Hubert and
Elmer sat next to each other, shaking
and trembling.

"Not by the hairs of our chinny-
chin-chins," squealed the pigs.

"Then I'll huff and I'll puff
and I'll blow your house in," said
the wolf.

Crash! In no time, the wolf
smashed his way through the walls
of Hubert's house!

"Yum, yum, fresh piggy for
dinner!" he cried, but Elmer and
Hubert got away and ran to Pete's
brick home.

"A w-w-wolf is chasing us and is going to break in here!" Elmer cried.

"This door is double-thick solid wood, with a strong bolt. He can't break it down," said Pete.

Sure enough, the wolf came banging on the door. "Let me in!"

"Not by the hairs on my chinny-chin-chin," Pete shouted.

"Then I'll huff and puff and I'll blow your house in!"

He huffed and puffed but could not get in.

"See?" Pete said to his brothers. "We are safe. I was just about to make some supper. Will you join me?" He lit a fire and put the pot on to boil.

Outside, the wolf ran headfirst at the door, sure it would crash open. But all he got for his troubles was a mighty sore head!

Then, the wolf spied the chimney.

"There's more than one way to get a pig!" he cried, climbing up onto the roof. "I'll just come down the chimney!"

"Stand back!" Pete warned his brothers as he took the cover off the boiling pot.

They listened as the wolf slid down the chimney and saw him land, with a mighty *plop!* in the pot of boiling water.

"Yyyeeeowwww!" the wolf cried.

Pete opened the front door, and the wolf ran out of the house and over the hills, far, far away.

"You can stay with me while you build your new houses," Pete told his brothers. "But this time you have to promise to work hard and build them strong and sturdy."

After that, Elmer and Hubert were never lazy again.

"You've learned an important lesson!" said the pigs' mother when she heard the story. "Hard work pays off."

Elmer and Hubert nodded. "It sure does!" they agreed.